crownless

Copyright © 2025 | [v0id.co]

1st Edition | Core Rules
Created by: Casey Owens

This is a work of fiction. Unless otherwise indicated, all the names, characters, businesses, places, events, and incidents in this book are either the product of the author's imagination or used in a fictitious manner. Any resemblance to actual persons, living or dead, or actual events is purely coincidental.

To my wife, my steadfast partner through every twist and turn, and to my daughter, my brightest chapter yet. This book exists because of the stories we share together.

I love you both beyond words.

Introduction

Crownless is a gritty, survival-driven roleplaying gamebook that thrusts players into a bleak, unforgiving world where power is fleeting, alliances are fragile, and death is never far behind. This is not a world of heroes or glory—this is a world of mud, blood, and desperation. Every choice you make is a gamble, and every step forward is a risk that could cost you everything.

In this Solo RPG gamebook, you don the muddy boots of a desperate individual struggling to carve out a fragile existence in the face of relentless hardship. Your character is not destined for greatness, nor are they protected by the hand of fate. They are a nameless survivor—a small cog in a world grinding towards ruin. It is up to you to navigate this ruthless reality, scavenging for resources, forging uneasy alliances, and outsmarting enemies both human and otherwise.

The world of Crownless is harsh and unrelenting. Kingdoms have fallen, their thrones now empty relics of a bygone era. Once-great empires lie in ruin, swallowed by decay and reclaimed by wilderness. The remnants of humanity are scattered, clinging to life in crumbling towns, isolated outposts, and shadowy camps. Lawlessness reigns supreme, and trust is a luxury few can afford.

This is a game of survival—not just of the body, but of the spirit. You will face tough decisions at every turn: betray your allies for a chance to live another day, or risk your life to uphold your fading morality? Sacrifice your safety to help a stranger, or take what little they have for yourself? In Crownless, there are no right answers—only the consequences of your actions.

As you journey through this fractured world, you will create your own narrative, weaving tales of triumph, failure, and bitter irony. The choices you make and the paths you tread will shape not only your character's fate but also the story of the broken world they inhabit.

How far are you willing to go to survive? What are you prepared to sacrifice to find a flicker of hope amidst the darkness? In Crownless, survival is victory, and the scars you bear are the only crown you'll ever wear.

Player Tools

Crownless is built on a unique roll-low d20 system; however, you will need a full set of polyhedral dice to play. This includes a d20, d12, d10, d8, d6, and d4. You can easily find cheap sets available at your local game store or online.

I recommend buying polyhedral dice sets in two different colors to allow for one designated set for the player character and one designated set for the combatant. This will help streamline play and roll for both at the same time.

I originally designed this system as a simple deviation from gamebooks that still provided the solo TTRPG experience in a travel-friendly way. In essence, the book acts as the GM steering you through your journey and encouraging the appropriate skill checks.

Character and enemy stats should be tracked on an index card, spare piece of paper, or even your phone's notes app. This comes down to personal preference, but you will still need a way to track everything for the best experience.

Take this core rulebook and some modules on an airplane, and with minimal setup you will find it can be played anywhere!

Adventuring

Every adventure in Crownless is designed as a self-contained module, giving players a fresh, dynamic experience each time they embark on a journey. This rulebook includes *Adventure Zero: Escape the Capital*.

Unlike other RPG titles, adventures in Crownless are designed as a standalone modules, featuring a funnel of interconnected locations or rooms. Players will navigate this funnel, choosing their actions and dealing with the consequences of them.

Pre-defined rooms or locations offer unique scenarios that require the player to make stat checks, rolling against their own Grit, Guile, or Instinct to overcome obstacles.

Encounters in each location can range from combat and traps to social situations and environmental hazards, providing a variety of challenges that test the character's abilities in different ways.

By playing different modules with the same character, you are able to quickly create a solo RPG campaign. If the challenge is too tough, replaying with an alternate character may decrease the target difficulty for the chosen module.

Characters

The world of Crownless is brutal, unforgiving, and stained with the struggles of those clinging to survival. In such a place, who you are defines whether you see another dawn or perish forgotten in the mud. Each character is a fragment of this broken world, shaped by hardship, betrayal, and fleeting moments of triumph.

Rather than crafting a hero from scratch, players will step into the shoes of pre-generated survivors, each with their own history, unique strengths, and carefully honed instincts. These characters are not blank slates but vivid personalities etched into the fabric of the setting, offering a rich tapestry of roleplaying opportunities.

Every choice you make will be influenced by the experiences and abilities of the character you embody. The Butcher might cleave through beasts with ease, while the Rat Catcher's nimbleness keeps them one step ahead of death. From the Disgraced Noble seeking redemption to the grim Excommunicant wielding faith as a shield, each survivor offers a distinct approach to the perils ahead.

The world is harsh, and survival is uncertain. Choose your survivor wisely—they are more than stats and dice rolls.

Butcher

Once a respected craftsman in a thriving town, the butcher was known for skillfully breaking down even the toughest cuts with surgical precision. When famine struck and civility crumbled, those same knives found new purpose. Flesh is flesh, after all, and the butcher quickly learned to survive by carving a path through the chaos. Their past is steeped in blood—both animal and human—and their survival instinct is as sharp as their cleaver.

- **Unique Perk**: *Predator's Edge* – Gains -2 shift on all attack rolls against animal or beast-type enemies.
- **Chosen Weapon**: *Cleaver* – A heavy blade that deals 1d10 slashing damage. If the first attack is successful, opponents continue to lose 1 HP per round for ongoing bloodloss.

Vitality
15 + 1d6

Stats:
Grit: 15
Guile: 8
Instinct: 10

Thief

Some tread lightly through the shadows, taking what they can without leaving a trace. The thief is a master of subtlety and deception, thriving in a world where quick hands and quicker wits are often the only tools for survival. Having slipped through the cracks of society long ago, they now skulk through ruins and strongholds, always looking for the next opportunity to stay one step ahead of death—or the law.

- **Unique Perk**: *Shadowstep* – Gains -2 shift on Dexterity rolls related to stealth, evasion, or hiding.
- **Chosen Weapon**: *Daggers* – Light and deadly, they grant a -1 shift to attack rolls and allow an additional attack once per turn if the first strikes. It deals 1d4 piercing damage for each strike.

Vitality
9 + 1d6

Stats:
Grit: 10

Guile: 16

Instinct: 13

Leech Collector

In the dank, forgotten swamps of the realm, the leech collector makes their living wading through filth and mire. Their hands are rough from years of plucking writhing leeches, their skin marred by countless bites. The poisons they've handled have seeped into their veins, making them tougher than most. To the untrained eye, the leech collector may seem grim and broken, but their connection to the natural world makes them a force to be reckoned with.

- **Unique Perk**: *Toxic Fortitude* – Has resistance to poison damage and -2 shift on rolls to resist disease.
- **Chosen Weapon**: *Bog Scythe* – A makeshift weapon, it grants a -2 shift to attack rolls and deals 1d8 slashing damage.

Vitality

13 + 1d6

Stats:

Grit: 13

Guile: 7

Instinct: 11

Disgraced Noble

Born into luxury and privilege, the noble lived a gilded life far removed from the struggles of the common folk. But no dynasty is eternal. Betrayal, scandal, or revolution brought their house crumbling down, and now they walk among the masses, a shadow of their former self. Despite their fall from grace, the noble's cunning and charisma remain intact, a glimmer of their former prestige shining through the grime.

- **Unique Perk**: *Noble's Command* – Once per encounter, can use their commanding presence to intimidate human enemies, forcing them to roll with a +3 shift on their next action.
- **Chosen Weapon**: *Rapier* – A finely crafted blade that grants a -1 shift to attack rolls and deals 1d6 slashing damage.

Vitality
11 + 1d6

Stats:
Grit: 11

Guile: 15

Instinct: 9

Rat Catcher

Crawling through gutters and sewers, the rat catcher has always been close to filth and decay. Armed with nothing but a rusty hook and a lifetime of grit, they've hunted vermin in the darkest places. What others see as pestilence, they see as opportunity, using the instincts honed in the muck to navigate this broken world. They know how to survive where others perish, and they've learned that even the smallest creatures can be an ally in dark times.

- **Unique Perk**: *Swarm Caller* – Once per encounter, can summon a swarm of rats to harass enemies, forcing them to roll with a +2 shift on their next attack.
- **Chosen Weapon**: *Rusty Hook* – A jagged weapon that deals 1d8 damage. On a roll of 1, the hook causes bleeding, dealing 1d4 damage per turn for two turns.

Vitality

14 + 1d6

Stats:

Grit: 10

Guile: 12

Instinct: 15

Excommunicant

Once a revered figure of the faith, the excommunicant fell from grace for reasons whispered in dark corners. Their robes are torn, their prayers unanswered, but the faint remnants of divine power still linger in their hands. They wander the broken world, a pariah seeking redemption—or revenge. Each step is a reminder of their lost position, and every encounter is a reminder that the world has forgotten their sacred oath.

- **Unique Perk**: *Unyielding Will* – Gains +2 shift on all wisdom rolls. They are immune to any form of intimidation or manipulation.
- **Chosen Weapon**: *Tarnished Censer* – A weighted weapon that deals 1d6 damage. When a critical hit is rolled, it releases a cloud of incense, shifting enemy rolls by +2 for a turn.

Vitality

12 + 1d6

Stats:

Grit: 8

Guile: 11

Instinct: 12

Combat

Combat in Crownless revolves entirely around Grit, the stat representing a character's physical endurance, combat skill, and raw resilience. It uses a *roll-low* d20 system, where the goal is to roll equal to or lower than the character's Grit to land a successful hit. Combat is gritty and dangerous, with no guarantee of survival even against weaker foes.

Steps of Combat

1. Attacker Rolls Against Grit
- When a character attacks, roll a d20 against their own Grit score. If the roll is equal to or lower than the Grit, the attack hits. If the roll is 1, the attack is a Critical Hit, dealing maximum damage for the weapon. If the roll is higher than the Grit, the attack misses.

2. Combatant Rolls Against Grit
- The player rolls for the enemy as well. Roll a d20 against the enemy's Grit score. If the roll is equal to or lower than the enemy's Grit, their attack hits. If the roll is higher, the enemy misses.

3. Damage Resolution
- If a hit lands, roll the attacker's damage dice (based on their *Chosen Weapon*). Subtract the damage from the defender's Vitality. If Vitality reaches 0, the defender is defeated.

Persuasion

Guile represents a character's wit, charm, and cunning, vital for navigating the social and strategic pitfalls of the Crownless world. While combat relies on Grit, Guile allows characters to manipulate, deceive, or maneuver their way through situations where raw strength won't suffice.

Guile checks come into play in scenarios such as convincing someone to lower their guard, passing as someone you're not to avoid conflict, lying to gain a tactical advantage, or creating distractions to escape a tense moment. In these moments, Guile is your character's greatest weapon, turning words and clever thinking into tools of survival.

To perform a Guile check, roll a d20 and compare the result to your Guile stat. If the roll is equal to or lower than the stat, the check is successful. A roll of 1 is a critical success, often yielding exceptional outcomes like a guard fully trusting your lies or gaining unexpected rewards. Conversely, a roll of 20 is a critical failure, resulting in consequences such as being caught in a lie or escalating tensions.

For instance, if your character tries to bluff their way past a suspicious guard with a Guile stat of 12, any roll of 12 or lower would succeed. A critical success might lead the guard to offer assistance, while a critical failure could result in hostility.

Stealth

Instinct embodies a character's ability to react swiftly, notice danger, and navigate the unpredictable world of Crownless. It reflects gut reactions, sharp perception, and the ability to avoid dangerous situations.

This trait is essential in moments where survival depends on stealth, keen observation, or reflexes. Characters use Instinct to identify traps or bypass a confrontation by sneaking by.

When rolling for an Instinct check, the process is simple: roll a d20 and compare the result to your Instinct stat. A roll equal to or lower than the stat indicates success, while a higher roll means failure.

A 1 is a critical success, representing an exceptional result such as spotting a hidden shortcut or uncovering a concealed resource. On the other hand, a 20 is a critical failure, which may lead to severe consequences like triggering a trap or falling prey to an ambush.

For example, a character attempting to sneak past a guard with an Instinct stat of 14 would need to roll a 14 or lower to go undetected and avoid combat.

Restoring Vitality

Once an adventure concludes, the character can fully restore their Vitality and prepare for the challenges ahead. Healing isn't just a matter of time; it reflects the moments spent tending to wounds, finding nourishment, and regaining resolve.

The character is assumed to have access to basic medical care, adequate food, and a safe place to rest, whether in a town, camp, or hidden refuge.

If your character dies during an adventure, their journey ends. There are no second chances. To continue, you must restart the current adventure from the beginning or select another module. Survival is unforgiving in the world of Crownless, and even a single misstep can bring an untimely end.

When restarting an adventure, the character begins anew with full Vitality and their starting equipment. Use what you've learned to navigate the dangers more carefully.

In some adventure modules, like *Through Thorn and Thicket*, you will have opportunities to harvest meat. Each portion can be consumed at the conclusion of a Zone to gain 1d6 Vitality.

Escape The Capitol

Adventure Zero

The King Is Dead...

His body still lies in the great hall, bleeding on the cold stone floor, surrounded by the shattered remnants of his court. The crown - once a symbol of strength and unity - sits broken beside him, it's golden spires twisted and bent. No one rushed to save him. No mourners dared to cry out.

Outside the palace walls, the city seethes. Hungry mobs fill the streets, their anger erupting like fires that leap from rooftop to rooftop. The nobles have barricaded themselves in their estates, sharpening their blades and muttering oaths of vengeance. The guards - once the King's most loyal protectors - scatter like rats, trading their armor for anonymity.

You are one of the countless souls caught in the maelstrom. Whether you mourn the King's death or curse his name matters little now. There are no safe havens left. The palace gates, once unyielding, now swing open like a maw inviting chaos to devour what remains.

Survival is the only law left in this broken city. The stay is to gamble with your life, and the odds grow slimmer with every passing hour. Somewhere, beyond the crumbling walls, the horizon beckons - an uncertain promise of escape and freedom. But the road out is treacherous. Will you carve your path out of the ruin or become another forgotten casualty?

Zone 1: The Throne Room

Blood pools beneath the king, mingling with the shards of his broken crown. Around you, the royal court has descended into chaos. Courtiers scream and flee, their elegant finery torn as they scramble over one another to escape. Soldiers bellow orders, their swords drawn as they cut down anyone they suspect of treason.

The air is heavy with the smell of iron and smoke. Flames creep along the edges of the vast chamber, licking at the once-grand tapestries. A royal guard, face twisted with fury and betrayal, points his blade at you, mistaking you for one of the conspirators.

You must move quickly. The palace doors are blocked by a mob of loyalists and looters. A narrow servants' passage to the east offers an escape, but it is no guarantee of safety. For a chance at survival, you must escape the throne room and find your way into the courtyard.

Character Choices
- Sneak past the guard using *Instinct*. If failed, combat begins with the Guard having first strike.
- Directly confront the Guard and gain initial combat strike.

King's Guard
Vitality: 14 | Grit: 10 | Damage: 1d6

Zone 2: The Palace Courtyard

The palace courtyard is a battleground, choked with dust and blood. The fountains that once sparkled with clear water now gush with red as limp bodies fall into their pools. Looters tear down banners, ripping apart anything of value.

To your left, a group of palace guards fight valiantly, but they are overwhelmed. To your right, a makeshift barricade blocks the main gated, constructed from overturned wagons and barrels. Beyond this lies the city, but you'll have to brave the chaos to reach it.

Above, smoke clouds the sky, blotting out the midday sun. The sounds of clashing steel and screaming voices echo in your ears. There's no turning back now - you're only hope is to make it through the courtyard and reach the armory. Fortunately, the palace guards haven't noticed you yet; however, a desperate looter has and he wants your weapon.

Character Choices
- Blend in with the looters using *Guile*. If failed, combat begins with the Desperate Looter having first strike.
- Directly confront the Desperate Looter and gain initial combat strike.

Desperate Looter
Vitality: 4 | Grit: 6 | Damage: 1d4

Zone 3: The Armory

The armory is a cavernous building, it's stone walls blackened with soot. Inside the remnants of a recent skirmish are clear: broken weapons litter the floor, and blood smears the walls. Fires still smolder in the corners, casting flickering shadows over racks of spears and swords.

Deserters and opportunists pick through the remains, filling their bags with weapons and supplies as the fire continues to suffocate the room. You realize that you must leave this room quickly before the flames block your escape.

As you quickly glance around the room, you realize there may be something useful here, but lingering too long will surely draw unwanted attention. You must work with haste to escape the armory and find the service tunnels. Sticking to the streets will certainly be too perilous.

Character Choices
- Search the armory quickly, using *Instinct* to avoid detection. Success lets you find a weapon upgrade (+1 to damage), while failure results in 1d4 burn damage.
- Leave without searching the armory and automatically escape the growing flames.

Roaring Flames
Lvl: 1 Trap | Damage: 1d4

Zone 4: The Service Tunnels

The service tunnels are a labyrinth of damp, narrow passageways beneath the city. The air is thick with the stench of sewage and decay, and the sound of dripping water echoes in the dark. Your footsteps are muffled by the slimy ground, but the chaos above feels amplified in the oppressive silence.

Rats skitter across the floor, their beady eyes glinting in the dim light of your torch. The distant sound of shouting and heavy footsteps suggests you were not the only one who thought to take this route. Fortunately, the steps are moving away from you.

You know from exploring these tunnels during childhood that they will exit at the lower market, a place that is familiar to you. You hope that the chaos hasn't reached that far yet, but expect the worst.

Character Choices
- *The Rat Catcher* is able to navigate the tunnels without fighting the pack of rats that have been attracted to the torch light.
- Other characters must engage in combat with the pack of rats, with the rats gaining first strike, before exiting.

Pack of Rats
Vitality: 6 | Grit: 6 | Damage: 1d4

Zone 5: The Lower Market

After emerging from the service tunnels, you find that the Lower Market is a shadow of its former self. Where merchants once hawked their wares to crowds bustled with life, now there is only destruction. Stalls lie in splinters, their goods looted or trampled into the dirt.

Fires smolder in overturned carts as survivors linger in the shadows, their hollow eyes following your every move. One figure, clutching a jagged blade, steps forward. "Back to take even more," they growl, their voice low and threatening.

You stand gauging your potential opponent and know that the Noble District is nearby, putting you one step closer to the Eastern Gate. If you can convince him that you aren't a threat, you know they will let you pass through unharmed.

Character Choices
- Convince the Hostile Survivor that you aren't a threat using a *Guile* check. If failed, combat begins with the survivor getting first attack.
- Directly confront the Hostile Survivor and gain initial combat strike.

Hostile Survivor
Vitality: 5 | Grit: 6 | Damage: 1d6

Zone 6: The Noble District

The cobblestone streets of the noble district are unnervingly quiet. Gilded mansions stand like tombs, their once ornate windows shattered and their gates torn from their hinges. The opulence here is now a mockery, stripped bare of their treasures by looters and vandals.

You catch movement on the rooftops - archers, scanning for anyone who doesn't belong. As peasants flee through the streets, their arrows whistle through the air, striking down anyone that comes into their line of sight. You'll have to move carefully to avoid their detection.

To the right, you notice that the overgrown gardens and alleys will provide adequate cover if you can reach them. If spotted to you will have to make a run for it to avoid their arrows.

Character Choices
- Use the overgrown gardens and alleys to remain unseen using an *Instinct* check.
- If the *Instinct* check is failed, you take 1d6 damage running to the nearby bridge as arrows fall from the sky to reach the Industrial District.

Rooftop Archers
Lvl: 2 Trap | Damage: 1d6

Zone 7: The Industrial District

The Industrial District has descended into a hellscape of fire and smoke. The forges and workshops have been abandoned mid-production, their machinery grinding to a halt. Sparks fly from shattered equipment, and molten metal pools on the ground, creating deadly hazards.

The street is seemingly abandoned aside from a hulking blacksmith wielding an abnormally large battle axe. Around him lies the bodies of several looters hacked to death, the remnants of their battle splattered across his leather apron and boots.

To make it to the Cathedral Square, you must get past this blacksmith, but he doesn't seem willing to compromise. Gaining an advantage by sneaking up on him may be the best option at survival - but it may be a tricky to pull off.

Character Choices
- Attempt to sneak up on the Blacksmith using an *Instinct* check. If successful, initial damage is doubled.
- If the *Instinct* check is failed, the Blacksmith gets the first attack as he notices you sneaking up on him.

Blacksmith
Vitality: 15 | Grit: 12 | Damage: 1d10

Zone 8: The Cathedral Square

The Cathedral looms over the square, it's bells tolling a dirge for the city. The news of the King's death has now reached the slums and things will become much more dangerous soon.

Outside the cathedral peasants plead for sanctuary, but the doors remain closed. Religious zealots patrol the square offering blessings for those who seek them, and striking down anyone that chooses to oppose them.

The air is thick with despair, but the atmosphere is a nice reprieve from the carnage you have faced thus far in your journey out of the city. As the chaos mounts, you can feel the weight of the crowd pressing against you, threatening to crush you if you don't act fast.

Character Choices
- Seek a blessing from the Religious Zealots using a *Guile* check. If successful, you recover 1d6 *Vitality*.
- If the *Guile* check is failed, there is no punishment and you must continue your journey without a blessing into the neighboring slums.

Religious Zealot
Lvl: 1 Blessing | Vitality: 1d6

Zone 9: The Slums

The Slums are a tangled web of misery and decay, a stark contrast to the gilded opulence of the noble district you left behind. The air hangs heavy with smoke and ash, casting everything in a suffocating gray haze. The narrow, crooked alleyways are lined with ramshackle huts made of rotting wood and scavenged metal, leaning precariously against one another like corpses propped upright.

The stench is overwhelming - a sickening mixture of unwashed bodies, burning refuse, and the sour tang of spilled blood. Occasionally, a faint cry or muffled scream pierces the silence, but no one stirs to investigate. Life here has been reduced to survival, and compassion is a luxury long abandoned.

As you make your way to the Eastern Gate, you catch the faint glint of a blade in the hand of a man lurking in the alleyway. As you pass, he walks behind you and demands you pay him to live.

Character Choices

- Fight the Starving Thief. Roll a d20 for each character's initiative to see who attacks first. The lower roll wins.

Starving Thief
Vitality: 4 | Grit: 6 | Damage: 1d4

Zone 10: The Eastern Gate

The Eastern Gate rises before you like a monument to futility - once an unyielding barrier of stone and steel, it now stands battered and broken. The great doors, once reinforced with iron, hang ajar, their wooden planks crack and splintered from the rioting mob's assault on the city that failed them.

The air here is electric, alive with the shouts and cries of the desperate throng that has claimed control of the gate. They are a motley crew of looters, vagrants, opportunists, and cutthroats.

Beyond the gate, the countryside beckons like a cruel mirage, its promise of freedom almost mocking in its proximity. A crude blockage is all that stands between you and your freedom - but you must fight to gain it.

You feel every muscle in your body tense as you approach, your instincts screaming that this is your last chance to survive. Will you break through the blockade or will you become another casualty of the ruined capitol?

Character Choices

- Fight through the Mob of Rioters. You gain first attack by charging at the blockade.

Mob of Rioters
Vitality: 15 | Grit: 10 | Damage: 1d6

The Road Ahead

The capitol falls away behind you, its towering walls now a distant silhouette against the choking haze of smoke. Each step away from the capitol feels like shedding a layer of filth, its cruelty, and its suffocating weight.

The cries of the mob at the gate have faded into the wind, replaced by an eerie, almost deafening silence that stretches across the open plains. The countryside feels alien. The land ahead is vast and untamed, a stark contrast to the crumbling, blood-soaked streets you left behind.

Above, the sun sinks toward the horizon, its fiery hues painting the sky ominous streaks of red and orange. The daylight wanes quickly, and with it comes the cold - a biting chill that seeps through your worn clothes and settles deep into your bones.

The road ahead offers no guarantees. Villages and hamlets dot the horizon, but the signs of struggle are evident even from afar: abandoned carts, distant columns of smoke, and fields left to rot. It's clear the sickness that gripped the city has begun to seep into the lands beyond.

You tighten your grip on your weapon, your fingers stiff from the cold and the weight of what lies ahead. The road beckons, winding into the unknown.

Printed in Great Britain
by Amazon